Everyone Is Invited to CHRISTMAS

A BIRTHDAY PARTY

for Jesus

by Susan Jones

Illustrated by Lee Holland

Good Books

New York, New York

In a tiny little hollow in the forest's farthest tree, Little Raccoon hears a tune. What could it be?

She peeks her head out of her hollow, and the sounds of the loveliest music and the cheeriest laughter make their way to her fluffy little ears.

Little Raccoon is not like other raccoons, or even other animals. She loves the daytime and her cozy, quiet tree.

But sometimes—just sometimes, she wishes she had a friend to play with!

Carefully and quietly, Little Raccoon follows the sounds of that jingling tune.

With a gust of wind, something flutters to her feet.

The wandering paper is for a celebration. It's a birthday party for Jesus!

"Who is Jesus?" Little Raccoon wonders. He must be very important.

As she follows the tune, thinking these thoughts to herself, Little Raccoon sees some rustling and some bustling in the bushes.

"Merry Christmas! Merry Christmas!" Little Hedgehog bursts from the bushes with arms open wide.

"I'm finding decorations for the party! Come with me! We need party hats and popcorn strings and ornaments and ribbons!"

"But I—" Little Raccoon starts, but Little Hedgehog scurries forward and chatters on, taking Little Raccoon by her hand.

They come to a clearing on the very edge of Little Raccoon's familiar forest. Creatures she's never seen are running around decorating, smiling, and singing! Singing to that tune!

Little Raccoon feels a big lump in her throat. What is the party about? Why is Jesus so special? Why does he have so many friends?

You're invited to Jesus's Birthday

"I don't think I'm invited," she says sadly. "I only *found* this invitation. It wasn't meant *for* me."

"But of course you are!"
squeals Little Hedgehog,
as loudly as can be.

"Everyone is invited
by Jesus!"

The forest animals gather around
Little Raccoon. "But when will
Jesus get here? Will he want me
at his party?"

Badger puts his arm around her and says, "Jesus is always here. His love *is* in our hearts, and we share it with others. Today and every day."

"Anyone can be Jesus's friend!" chimes in Little Bunny, who has bounced up from under the pile of gifts by the tree.

"It's true!" Little Hedgehog smiles brightly. "And you can be our friend, too!"

With her heart filled,
surrounded by her newfound
friends, Little Raccoon feels
a warmth and happiness like
nothing she's ever felt before.

On Jesus's birthday, she received the gifts of friendship and love that she can accept and share forever.